Lizzie McGuire

Freaked Out

Adapted by Alice Alfonsi
Based on the series created by Terri Minsky
Part One is based on a teleplay written
by Melissa Gould.
Part Two is based on a teleplay written
by Douglas Tuber & Tim Maile.

Watch it on
Disney CHANNEL
abc kids

Disney PRESS

VOLO

New York

PART ONE

CHAPTER ONE

The freakiest day of Lizzie McGuire's life didn't start out very freaky at all. In fact, it began like any other totally normal school day.

Lizzie got up, brushed her teeth, washed her face, and fixed her hair.

Next came the clothes. Achieving maximum fashion perfection could be a trying process. But that morning, Lizzie nailed it in record time. The trick, she found, was first deciding on one piece of clothing, then choosing others to go with it.

This morning, she'd started with a silver-studded jeans skirt, paired it with a metallic belt, then topped it with a clingy, long-sleeved pink jersey.

Totally stylin', thought Lizzie, checking herself out in the mirror. Then she frowned. There was a small orange spot on the front of her shirt.

Uh-oh, maybe not so stylin'.

She licked her finger and rubbed. But the smudge wouldn't budge!

Just when you think your outfit is perfect, you find last week's pizza stain.

Lizzie examined the stain a bit closer.

Which is kind of weird because it should've been washed in *last* week's laundry.

Whatever, thought Lizzie.

She began to rummage through her closet for a new top. But the next one she chose had an ink mark on the sleeve. And the one after that had a juice stain on the collar.

One by one, she jerked the shirts off their hangers. Each one had some sort of disfiguring stain, spot, or wrinkle. And some of her favorite skirts and pants were in the same sorry shape!

Which means something bizarro is going on with my wardrobe, and I don't mean my blacks don't match.

This could only be the work of one person, Lizzie realized—her twerpy little rodent-breath brother! With window-rattling rage, she opened her mouth and yelled the dreaded name:

"Ma-a-a-a-tt!"

Then Lizzie stomped out of her bedroom and into the hall.

"You rang?" Matt asked, sliding over to her in his socks.

"What have you done to my clothes?" she demanded.

Matt opened his eyes as wide as an innocent

little lamb's. "Why, nothing," he said in his I-have-no-idea-what-you're-talking-about voice.

Lizzie wasn't buying it. She pointed to the pizza stain on her shirt. "Well, then, what is this?"

Matt shrugged. "Proof that you're a slob, I guess."

"You are such vermin!" cried Lizzie. "Why can't you just stay out of my stuff and quit invading my privacy!"

"How is taking your dirty, disgusting, nasty clothes out of the hamper and putting them back in your closet 'invading your privacy'?" asked Matt.

The nerve! "Just stop ruining my life!" Lizzie yelled.

"Quit ruining mine!" Matt yelled right back.

Ruining *his*? thought Lizzie. "What are you talking about?" she asked.

"You never give me my phone messages, you're always taking my lunch to school instead of yours, and you hog the bathroom," said Matt.

"News flash, Matt. You don't *get* any phone messages. And I took your lunch to school *one* time by accident, and I don't hog the bathroom any more than you do."

Well, maybe a little.

Lizzie threw her hands up. "Fine," she said.

"Fine," Matt said right back.

In the very next instant, Lizzie and Matt cried together, "I'll stay out of your life!"

Then they both turned and went back to their bedrooms, slamming their doors behind them.

Lizzie was so angry, she didn't notice the change right away. But as she stomped farther into the room, she realized things weren't quite right.

For starters, she'd just walked *away* from Matt. But now he was standing right in front of her.

Wait! Lizzie thought. That's not Matt. That's a mirror. *I'm* standing in front of it, and *Matt* is staring back!

No. It can't be, she thought.

Slowly, she lifted her hand to her mouth. At the exact same time, the reflection of Matt lifted *its* hand to *its* mouth.

Why do i suddenly look like Matt?

Confused, Lizzie looked around. Action figures, robot toys, and sports equipment cluttered the room.

Hey, wait a minute, she thought. What is this?

This isn't my room!

Lizzie jumped away from the mirror, then back again. But the reflection didn't change. She knew who she was. She was Lizzie McGuire. So why was the mirror reflecting *toad-boy's* face?!

Ohmigosh! i *am* Matt!

Suddenly, Lizzie heard a girl scream in the

next room. She ran out of Matt's bedroom and came face-to-face with—*herself*!

"Ahhhhh!" Lizzie and Matt screamed together.

"Kids!" called Mrs. McGuire from downstairs. "Stop your fighting!"

"But I'm you!" cried Lizzie from Matt's body.

"And I'm you!" cried Matt from Lizzie's body.

"Give me back my body, worm!" Lizzie demanded, shaking her . . . well, actually Matt's . . . grubby little finger at her brother, who suddenly looked an awful lot like HER-SELF!

"Yeah," said Matt, waving around Lizzie's manicured hand, "like I want to be a stupid girl!"

"Okay," said Lizzie, trying not to panic, "what do we do?!"

"Stop, drop, and roll!" suggested Matt, spinning his . . . errr . . . *Lizzie's* . . . arms to make his point.

"No, Matt, that's fire safety!" said Lizzie. She closed her . . . ummm . . . *Matt's* . . . eyes and tried to remain calm.

Think, she told herself. Just think this through logically. As if *that* were possible.

"How did this happen?" Lizzie asked. But when she talked, Matt's voice came out. This was way too freaky to comprehend!

"I don't know!" screeched Matt in Lizzie's voice. "One minute I'm switching your shampoo with shaving cream, and the next minute . . . I'm you!"

"But before that, we were fighting," recalled Lizzie.

"We told each other to stay out of our lives, right?" said Matt.

Yes, thought Lizzie, dweeb-boy is right.

"And we said it at the exact same time!" She thought for another moment. "So, let's say it again and see if we switch back," she said. "On my count. One, two, three—"

"Stay out of my life!" they cried together.

For a second, they just stood in the hallway, staring at each other.

"Well?" they asked at the same time.

Lizzie didn't feel any different. She *still* felt like *Matt*.

Now what? she wondered, staring into her own face, which was currently occupied by an unwanted guest . . . a guest who seemed to be suddenly distracted by her footwear.

"How high are these shoes?" Matt asked, pointing down at Lizzie's stacked, cork-soled mules. "They're kind of cool," he said, teetering a bit as he bent over to take a closer look at them. Then he straightened Lizzie's body to its full height, stretched out Lizzie's arms like

Frankenstein, and began to tramp around. "I am Giant Matt. Fear me!"

"Matt!" screeched Lizzie, horrified. "This is serious!"

As she yelled, Lizzie became aware of something other than the fact that she sounded just like her twerp-boy brother. There was an icky taste in her mouth (well, really *Matt's* mouth). "And when is the last time you brushed your teeth?" she demanded. Her "new set" of chompers felt all slimy and grungy. She picked at them and found a big glob of jelly bean stuck to a molar. "*Yuck.* That's disgusting!"

The phone rang. Lizzie ignored it. "What are we going to do?" she asked her brother. "I really don't want to be you!"

"And I really, *really* don't want to be you," said Matt. "Besides, how are we going to explain this to people?"

The phone stopped ringing and Mrs. McGuire called up the stairs, "Lizzie—Miranda and Gordo are on the phone!"

Lizzie ducked into Matt's room, which she guessed was her room now, given the recent turn of events (gross!), and grabbed the cordless receiver. With Matt's raggedy-nailed index finger, she pressed the TALK button.

"Um . . ." she began, then stopped. What should I say? she asked herself. Sure, she was *dying* to blurt out the truth to her two best friends, but they'd never believe her—especially if they heard it from a voice that sounded like toad-boy's.

Finally, she said, "Lizzie's a little busy at the moment."

That was true, too . . . kind of. In the hall-way, Matt was running Lizzie's body around like a remote-control toy. He marched this way, then that—trying to manage his new-found height.

Lizzie's best friend, David "Gordo" Gordon, wasn't happy to hear Lizzie couldn't come to the phone. Especially from a voice that sounded like Matt's.

"Why?" Gordo asked. "What'd you do to her?"

"Switch her shampoo with shaving cream again?" said Lizzie's other best friend, Miranda Sanchez.

"Me? No," Lizzie said in Matt's voice. "Let's just say, Lizzie's not quite herself this morning. She's a lot like . . . *me*."

"Oh," said Miranda. "You mean short and annoying?"

Annoying is right! Lizzie thought. While she was trying to talk on the phone, Matt was there, poking and pinching his own body, which Lizzie was now occupying, apparently loving the fact that he could torture it and not feel a thing. But Lizzie, who was trapped inside, was not enjoying her brother's little pseudo scientific examination of pinching and prodding one bit. It hurt! *Ouch!*

Meanwhile, Gordo was still laughing at Miranda's joke. "Ha-ha. That's funny."

Lizzie couldn't take any more of Matt's poking and prodding. "Actually," she told her friends, remembering that she sounded like Matt, "I'll have her call you back. Bye!"

After hanging up, Lizzie barked at her brother, "Cut it out! This is the worst thing that's ever happened to me."

That's when Lizzie realized she wasn't *only* looking *at* herself. She was looking *up* at herself. So this is how Matt saw her . . . *heh-heh.*

"And you're *short*!" she added.

"At least I have good hair," said Matt,

touching his short-cropped spikes that Lizzie was currently sporting while she was trapped in her brother's body. Then Matt touched Lizzie's silky, shoulder-length blond hair and said, "I don't know what to do with all this stuff." Then an evil look came across his face and, pretending his fingers were scissors, he said, "Maybe I'll just chop it off!"

"Don't. You. Dare!" Lizzie screeched.

Just then, Mr. McGuire came out of his bedroom. "You better get a move on, kids," he told them as he walked toward the stairs with his newspaper. "You're going to be late for school."

Matt and Lizzie looked at each other. Or at themselves. Or . . . oh, whatever!

"Dad didn't even notice," whispered Lizzie. Then she gasped. "Matt. Did he say *school*?" No, no, no! she thought. This *can't* be happening.

But it *was* happening. And even though it felt as though she'd been in this bizarro situation for *years*, the freakiest day of Lizzie McGuire's life was just getting started.

CHAPTER TWO

Ten minutes later, Lizzie and Matt were huddled together on the living-room couch. Blankets covered their shoulders. Thermometers hung from their mouths.

A few feet away, Mr. and Mrs. McGuire whispered to each other. "You really think they're *both* sick?" Mrs. McGuire asked.

"Well," said Mr. McGuire, "Lizzie never pulls stunts like this. But Matt?"

Mrs. McGuire nodded. "You take him, and I'll take her."

"Got it," said Mr. McGuire.

Mr. McGuire pulled the thermometer out of Matt's mouth, and Mrs. McGuire pulled the second one out of Lizzie's.

"Okay," said Mrs. McGuire, standing in front of her children, "let's see what we got."

Mr. McGuire read his thermometer: "98.6 degrees."

"I got 98.6 degrees, too," said Mrs. McGuire.

"Normal," said Mr. McGuire.

Mr. and Mrs. McGuire shared a confused look. "They didn't even try to fake it," she whispered.

"Matt?" said Mr. McGuire.

"You rang?" answered Matt—in Lizzie's body.

"I believe I said *Matt*," Mr. McGuire snapped.

Whoops, thought Lizzie, *I'm* Matt. That's *me*!

"But we're sick," she quickly croaked in Matt's voice, which sounded just as annoying to her now as it did when Matt was choosing the words. How could she live with herself sounding like a whiny toad for the rest of her life? Well, or at least until her, no, *his*, voice changed!

Beside her, Matt coughed a few times. "See?" he said. He can't even cough like me, Lizzie thought. This is *so* not going to work.

"I don't feel well," said Lizzie, trying to sound like Matt by using that bogus innocent tone her brother liked to use. "I totally don't feel like myself today."

"Matt," Mrs. McGuire said to Lizzie, "we didn't buy that when you were trying to get out of that history test, and we're not buying it today."

But today's actually a really good day to buy it!

"And, Lizzie," Mrs. McGuire continued to Matt, "I don't know why *you're* pretending to be sick, but I'm disappointed that you would go to such lengths to avoid whatever it is at school that you're not telling me about."

Not telling you about?! Okay, that's it— i'm telling Mom.

"It's like this—" Lizzie began, leaning forward. Only Mr. McGuire didn't know it was Lizzie who was trying to do the explaining. And thinking it was Matt (who it sure looked like), he cut her off.

"—I'm talking to your *sister*, Matt. Not you!" he said, obviously frustrated.

Arrrggghhh! Lizzie wanted to scream. Talk about *frustration*!

But i *am* his sister!

"Lizzie," Mrs. McGuire asked Matt meaningfully, "is there anything I ought to know?"

This has to stop, thought Lizzie, watching her own mother speak to "her." This whole out-of-body-experience thing is getting *real* old *real* fast!

Lizzie tried to explain again. "What I'm trying to say is—"

Suddenly, Lizzie's own face (currently possessed by a little demon called Matt) turned to her and, sounding just like her, snapped, "Can it, fungus. Mom's right."

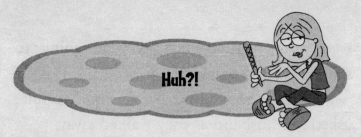

Huh?!

"Sorry, Mom," Matt continued, now trying hard to act like Lizzie. "Matt, he's so clever, he dared me to play sick. And, I, being Lizzie, wasn't as convincing as I could've been. We'll be ready for school in a couple of minutes."

Mr. McGuire and Mrs. McGuire shared another confused look.

"He *dared* you?" Mrs. McGuire asked. "Since when do you listen to your brother?"

Matt shrugged and said, "He *is* the smartest boy on the whole planet."

Lizzie groaned. Hearing *that* sentence come out of her own mouth actually *did* make her feel sick!

But Mr. McGuire and Mrs. McGuire weren't listening to any more excuses. As far as they were concerned, their kids were going to school today. Period.

"What has gotten into them?" Mrs. McGuire asked her husband as they walked away.

Mr. McGuire just shook his head. "I haven't a clue."

As soon as their parents were out of earshot, Matt spoke . . . from Lizzie's body. "Well, then," he said, "I guess we'll have to go about our day as normally as possible, and we'll try and figure out how to switch back when we get home from school."

"There's just one thing," said Lizzie (though anyone who didn't know better would think Matt was saying it).

"Talk to me," said Matt.

Lizzie placed a hand from the body she was now occupying onto the shoulder of the one she had so unfairly been evicted from and said, "Don't. Ruin. My. Life."

"Me? Ruin your life?" scoffed Matt, waggling Lizzie's own manicured fingers at her. "Why, whatever do you mean?"

Then Matt launched off the couch, finally tossing away the "sick" blanket he'd wrapped Lizzie's "old" body in.

Lizzie gasped when she got a look at what he was wearing. Normally she wouldn't care how grungy he looked. But today, he wasn't only wearing her clothes but also her body. And nobody knew any better. They would think *she* was—*gasp!*—a slob!

Gone were the totally stylin' clothes she'd chosen to wear earlier. Her cool jean skirt and clingy pink jersey had been replaced with a pair of faded plaid pants, an oversized old T-shirt, and a jockish warm-up jacket. A completely style*less* ensemble!

"I wasn't wearing that this morning!" Lizzie shouted at her brother.

"Personally," said Matt, from Lizzie's hideously outfitted body, "I think you wear your clothes a little too tight. But, if you insist, I'll go upstairs and change."

"Just wear something *normal*, okay?" she pleaded.

Then she pulled her own "sick" blanket all the way over her head. Why couldn't she just stay under there all day?

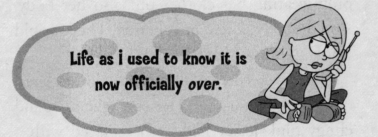

Life as i used to know it is now officially *over*.

As soon as Matt, in his new Lizzie-form, reached Lizzie's bedroom, he marched over to the dresser.

Now, what would "Lizzie" wear to school? he asked himself.

He spotted a pink feather boa and put it on.

That's sort of cool, he thought.

Next, he pulled Lizzie's blond hair straight up into a high ponytail.

Then he grabbed a doll sitting on the dresser and plopped it on Lizzie's head.

"Me likee. Me likee," yapped Matt, making the doll dance until it toppled over.

Next door, in Matt's room, Lizzie was standing in front of a mirror, too.

My mission, thought Lizzie, is to tame wild-boy's ridiculously spiky hair!

First, she tried to get a comb through it. And failed.

Next, she covered Matt's entire head with hair gel, put a shower cap on it, and let it sit for three minutes. When she took off the cap, she was pleased. The hideous hair seemed to be staying down.

But a second later, it sprang back up again!

Okay, thought Lizzie, I may have to go through an entire day in Matt's body. But I *do not* have to put up with hair that looks like Astroturf!

"That's it," said Lizzie. "The gloves are coming off!"

Meanwhile, back in Lizzie's bedroom, Matt had found a bunch of wigs in a box marked HALLOWEEN COSTUMES.

He spotted a big blond Afro wig and pulled it on.

Wow, thought Matt—retro!

He thought this look would really do wonders for his sister's image at her junior high school. Then again, the way she treated him, he figured he didn't owe her any favors.

"Way too cool for my geek sister," he murmured. Then he shook the blond 'fro this way and that, gave himself the peace sign, and pulled it off.

At the same moment, in Matt's room, Lizzie was pouring ingredients into a cup.

A little bit of gel.

A little bit of wax.

A little bit of glue.

And voilà! Lizzie thought, mixing it all up with one end of Matt's comb. The perfect hair de-spiking formula!

Back in Lizzie's bedroom, Matt found a vampire wig of straight black hair in the Halloween costumes box. He spotted a cowboy hat in the box, too, and plopped it on top of the wig.

Matt was truly impressed with himself. He'd invented a whole new look. I'll call it "Goth-western," he said to himself. This new look for Lizzie was totally original. And it was even cooler than the blond Afro!

But then Matt changed his mind.

His geeky sister *still* didn't deserve to look this awesome. So he pulled off the wig and the hat.

Lizzie, of course, had no clue what was happening back in her bedroom. She was too busy smearing her new de-spiking formula all over Matt's head.

Once she covered toad-boy's stupid spikes, she combed the greasy mess down into place. And this time, it actually stayed!

Yes! Lizzie thought. Wild-boy's beastly hair is finally tamed!

Now, thought Lizzie, time for the next item on the agenda. *Clothes.*

She tapped her chin. How am I going to *re-dress* my hoodlum brother?

* * *

Finally, Mrs. McGuire shouted up the stairs for Matt and Lizzie to hurry up. They were both about to miss their buses.

Inside Matt's room, Lizzie glanced at the mirror one last time to check out the "new look" she'd given her brother. The 1950s sitcoms like *Leave It to Beaver* had been her inspiration.

Not bad, Lizzie thought, considering what she had to work with.

Next door, inside *Lizzie*'s room—and body—Matt was thinking the very same thing.

The new look he'd chosen for his sister wasn't quite as far-out as he would have liked. But it was far enough.

Then, at the exact same moment, both sister and brother shrugged and said, "It'll do."

CHAPTER THREE

At Lizzie's school, Miranda walked Gordo to his locker. To pass the time, she asked him one of those "desert island CD" questions.

Big mistake, realized Miranda the second Gordo started to answer.

"If I were stuck on a desert island," Gordo told her, "chances are my top five CD choices would be the *least* of my concerns."

Gordo grabbed his binder and slammed his locker door shut.

"It was just a question," Miranda said in exasperation. "Sheesh, do you always have to be so . . . practical?"

"Well it's *practicality*, not my CD collection, that would get me off the island," Gordo pointed out.

As Miranda rolled her eyes, she glimpsed someone moving down the crowded hallway. For some reason—maybe that desert-island-CD question—the person reminded Miranda of all those disco songs from the 1970s that old people like her parents listened to.

Then Miranda took a longer look and gasped. "Oh. My. Gosh."

Seeing the stunned look on Miranda's face, Gordo turned to see what had made her wince.

"Oh," he said. "You. Weren't. Kidding." Then he winced, too.

Lizzie McGuire was strutting down the hall.

Occasionally, she'd pause to correct her balance because her platform shoes were so high, she could hardly walk in them. And her outfit was the most embarrassing thing Gordo had ever seen her wear to school.

She'd put a silver-foil stamped shirt over silver metallic pants, then hung a long, flower-print robe with a black boa collar over the whole thing.

And then there were feathers. Lots and lots of feathers.

Gordo looked again—mostly because he couldn't believe it. *Yep.* It was true, he realized. She'd clipped *feathers* to her partly braided hair.

Suddenly, Gordo revised what he'd thought earlier. This wasn't the most embarrassing outfit he'd seen Lizzie wear to school. It was the most embarrassing outfit he'd seen *anybody* wear to school.

Their fellow students obviously agreed.

They were pointing and laughing. But Lizzie just kept walking and smiling.

She even fell off her platforms and went down, *oof!*, right in the middle of the hall. But she didn't seem to mind. In fact, she acted like it was all a big joke. She just picked herself up again. And, with a big smile, she continued to strut.

For the first time Gordo could remember, Lizzie didn't appear to notice—or even care—what anyone else thought. Of course, none of them could know that Lizzie wasn't really Lizzie today, but her little brother, *Matt!*

"So, guys," said Matt, walking right up to Lizzie's two best friends. "Where's our first class?"

"Lizzie!" cried Miranda, appalled. "What are you . . . I mean, how can you . . . ?"

Gordo spoke up. "I think what Miranda's trying to say is, what were you thinking when you got dressed this morning? You look like Elton John."

"That's *Sir* Elton John," Matt said ferociously. "And I *like* these shoes. Where's bad?"

Miranda and Gordo shared an uncertain look.

Matt was getting nervous. He really wanted to pull this off. "When's lunch?" he quickly chirped with a big smile. "I'm gettin' kind o' hungry."

Miranda narrowed her eyes. "Okay, *who* are you and what have you done with my best friend?"

Matt imitated Lizzie's best "I'm in deep thought" expression by biting his (well, really Lizzie's) lip. He'd have to come up with *some* explanation for his disco-queen outfit.

"Well," he finally said, "Matt, in a brilliant ruse, decided to donate all my clothes to a traveling circus. So, this is all I have left."

Miranda nodded.

So did Gordo.

They actually bought it!

"Why don't your parents just send him to military school?" suggested Miranda, before heading toward class.

"I've never thought of that!" Matt cried. But as he chased after Miranda, Matt silently made a note to himself: keep this girl and her military school ideas *away* from the 'rents!

Then Matt fell off Lizzie's shoes—and flat on his face—*again*.

While Matt was making Lizzie a *spectacle*, Lizzie was trying to make Matt *invisible*.

She sat at Matt's little desk in his elementary school classroom, hands neatly folded.

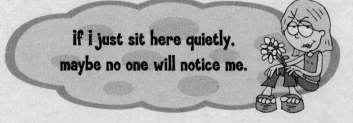

if i just sit here quietly, maybe no one will notice me.

Too late, she thought as she noticed Matt's friend Melina approach.

"Brilliant," said Melina. "Totally brilliant."

Lizzie looked around the classroom, then back at Melina. "Are you talking to me?" she asked.

Melina looked the person who she thought was Matt up and down. His hair was greased down and neatly combed. And his clothes looked like they came right out of a 1950s TV show: pressed khaki pants; a brown-plaid, long-sleeved button-down; a V-neck sweater-vest; and penny loafers.

"Dressing like a nerd . . . putting soap bubbles in the school fountain," said Melina, shaking her head. "Amateur, but that should buy you at least a few minutes before you get in trouble."

Standing near Melina, Lanny nodded enthusiastically. Then the two took their seats next to Lizzie.

Get in trouble?! i'm lucky i even knew how to find this class.

"But how could I be in trouble?" Lizzie asked Melina. "I've been sitting here the entire time."

"Totally amateur excuse, too," replied Melina to Lizzie. "We'll work on your alibi for when you're called to the principal's office."

Lanny nodded again.

"Why would I be called to the principal's office?" Lizzie asked nervously. "I haven't done anything. I can't be in trouble."

Just then, the school secretary's voice came over the public-address system. "Good morning, students. Thanks to a particular ne'er-do-well, there will be no eating lunch by the front lawn fountain today."

Moans and groans rose from the classroom.

"That being said," continued the secretary's amplified voice, "will Matt McGuire please report to the principal's office?"

Suddenly, all the students in class broke out in applause.

"The principal's office?" said Lizzie in shock. "But I'm innocent! I don't even know *where* the principal's office is."

Lanny, thinking Lizzie was just Matt playing up this new nerd role, couldn't help but crack up. Melina just smiled. "Oh, Matt," she said. "Such a kidder."

This is so unfair. At least at home when Matt gets in trouble, he deserves it. . . . This is a conspiracy against my brother!

CHAPTER FOUR

Back in the halls of Hillridge Junior High, Miranda was totally perplexed.

Ethan Craft was the hottest hottie in school. He was so hot, Lizzie usually couldn't do more than stammer a few words around the guy.

But today, during their first class, Lizzie started chatting with Ethan. And for some unknown reason, he was hanging on her every word!

So *what* could they be talking about? Dying

of curiosity, Miranda crept up behind the two of them as they walked out of class together.

". . . Yeah, and I got this from when I fell off my motorbike," Ethan was saying. He pointed out a small scar on his arm for Lizzie to see.

"Oh, sweet!" Matt cried. "So, did it ooze pus or blood?"

"Little bit of both," Ethan said to Matt.

"Did it get all scabby?" asked Matt. "I just love to pull back scabs."

"You like that?" asked Larry Tudgeman, who was walking alongside them. He pulled up his pant leg and pointed to his knee. "I got this bruise on me one time, and it went from black to yellow, then back to black."

Matt nodded. "Yeah, one time I got a bruise—I was jumping onto this Velcro wall that me and my dad made—it was so gross that—"

Miranda stopped listening and turned to Gordo. He'd been walking along beside Miranda, listening in, too.

"Scabs, bruises, scars," said Miranda. "I mean, do we need to do an *intervention* or something?"

"Um, I know that this is going to sound weird," said Gordo, "but Lizzie's acting pretty cool. I mean, she seems so comfortable with herself."

Miranda watched Lizzie, not knowing, of course, that she was really watching Matt, who was finishing up the story and seemed really relaxed and happy. Ethan and Larry were nodding their heads, totally into the conversation.

"It is weird," admitted Miranda. "I mean, the one day where she looks terrible, she has what looks like the best conversation she's ever had with Ethan Craft."

Hmmm, thought Miranda. "Maybe I should dress like her tomorrow," she said.

Gordo sighed and shook his head. *Two* best friends who dressed like Elton John he *didn't* need.

"See you at lunch, Lizzie," Ethan called before heading off down the hall. "Later."

"Yeah. Me, too," echoed Larry.

"Later," said Matt.

Miranda was about to approach her friend, when Kate Sanders, queen of mean, beat her to it. The she-beast cheerleader stormed right up to Matt and started snarling.

"Let me tell you something, Lizzie," Kate said in her usual superior manner. "The next time you plan on stealing my lunch date with Ethan . . . well, you better not."

"I didn't steal your lunch date," said Matt with a shrug.

Watching nearby, Miranda couldn't believe

Lizzie was being so cool and calm! Kate certainly wasn't. She got right into Matt's Lizzie-face and demanded, "Then how come I just heard Ethan say he'll see you at lunch?"

"Maybe because he is going to See. Me. At lunch," said Matt, pointing to Lizzie eyes, then herself, then her mouth. Then he shot Kate a look that said, "Duh."

Miranda nearly burst out laughing!

Kate's eyes narrowed. "If you mess up my lunch date with Ethan, you'll never eat lunch in this school again. Got it?"

Matt imitated Lizzie's best eye roll, then walked away. "I don't care."

"Freak!" called Kate as Matt joined Miranda and Gordo.

But even Kate's parting shot didn't seem to bother Lizzie. Miranda was very impressed.

"Lizzie, you totally told Kate off," Miranda said to Matt as they climbed the stairs to their next class. "I am totally dressing like you tomorrow."

That's when Matt lost his balance *again*. Miranda and Gordo turned to see the person they *thought* was their best friend rolling down the steps and collapsing into a heap at the bottom.

But Matt was okay. And after he'd regained his composure, he even advised Miranda. "Maybe you should rethink the shoes."

Except for the occasional dive off Lizzie's platforms, Matt was really having a great time with the junior-high thing.

His first class had gone really well, and now he was ready for his second.

He was about to sit down at Lizzie's desk when Kate kicked the seat out from under him. And instead of hitting the seat, Lizzie's rear hit the floor.

Kate smirked as Gordo and Miranda rushed forward.

"Lizzie, are you okay?" asked Gordo.

Matt answered, "I seem to be spending a lot of time on the ground."

"Yeah," said Miranda, "but Kate just made you look like a total idiot!"

"That's fine," said Matt, glancing up at the smirking Sanders she-beast.

Then Matt did a little smirking himself. "She has no idea who she's dealing with."

Meanwhile, over at the elementary-school lunchroom, Lizzie walked uncertainly on Matt's short legs. All the tables and chairs seemed a little small.

When she spotted Lanny and Melina, she went over to their table and sat down.

"I just got *detention*," she told them, collapsing into a defeated lump. "People like me don't do well in detention. I didn't even put the bubbles in the fountain. This is so unfair."

Melina and Lanny looked at each other in confusion.

"Um, hello," said Melina. "That's the way it always works. We always get in trouble for stuff. Sometimes for stuff we didn't even do. So Principal Alder yells a little, then sends us on our way. The predictability is actually sort of comforting."

Lanny nodded silently.

"Oh, really?" said Lizzie, mimicking Matt's sarcastic tone as best she could. "You find three weeks' detention comforting?!"

Melina dropped her milk carton. And Lanny spit out his apple juice.

"*Three weeks'* detention!" Melina cried in shock. "But that never happens! Well, only for really bad stuff, but still. You're right. That is totally unfair."

Thank you!

"I'll tell you what's even more unfair," said Lizzie. "I follow the rules. I never get into trouble. I do my homework, and I'm never late for class! I am a good kid!"

"Okay, this is *us* you're talking to," Melina said. "What is going on?"

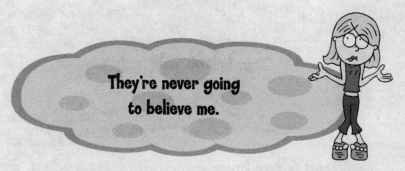

They're never going to believe me.

"I'll tell you what's going on! I'm *Lizzie!*" she blurted out. "Somehow Matt and I switched places this morning, and we don't know how to switch back!"

Lanny and Melina's eyes widened. Then Lanny threw a look at Melina, and she nodded.

"Okay, Matt—I mean, Lizzie," said Melina. "Here's what we're going to do—"

Lizzie jumped in. "You actually *believe* me?"

Lanny nodded.

Lizzie wanted to jump for joy!

They believe me!

"Truth is, we knew something was up when you walked past Clark Benson without sneezing in his pudding," Melina confessed.

Lizzie looked confused, and Melina nodded her head in the direction of another table. A nerdy-looking boy sat there, eating his chocolate pudding as if it were the first time he could enjoy it in months.

So my brother was *sneezing* in that poor kid's pudding cup? thought Lizzie. Every day?

Wow. Matt's really gross.

Over at the junior high, Matt marched right over to Kate Sanders after class.

"So, Kate," said Matt in a totally cool, calm Lizzie voice. "That little stunt that you pulled—kicking the chair out from underneath me? A little amateur."

"But I didn't do that," said Kate, acting totally innocent. "You must be confusing me with someone else."

"Oh, Kate, Kate, Kate," said Matt as they approached Kate's locker, "you have no idea who you're dealing with. I may *look* like sweet, innocent little Lizzie McGuire. But that'll be your undoing."

Kate waved her hand at Lizzie, totally unimpressed. "Please," she said.

"I'm just saying, when you least expect it—*expect* it. . . . It could be *now*," said Matt, walking away. "Or it could be *now*. . . . Or it could be now. . . . Or not." Then Matt pointed at Kate and said, "Later."

Kate rolled her eyes and shook her head. Lizzie McGuire was obviously the *last* person Kate would ever fear. And that's exactly what Matt was counting on!

As he walked up to Miranda and Gordo, he

did a classic Lizzie head toss and said, "Watch and learn."

As Kate opened her locker door, half a dozen slimy frogs from the science lab leaped out at her.

With a terrified scream, she started running down the hall. Which was exactly what Matt had expected. Because he had placed a pile of banana peels on the floor!

Kate's stacked black boots slipped and sent her flying into the nearest doorway. That's when the bucket of chili Matt had rigged came pouring down all over her head.

"Lizzie!" Kate screamed.

But nobody actually heard her. All the kids in the hall—including Gordo and Miranda—were laughing too hard!

CHAPTER FIVE

After lunch at the elementary school, Lizzie walked back toward Matt's classroom.

"How'd it happen exactly?" asked Melina.

"I have no idea," Lizzie answered. "I mean, one minute Matt and I were fighting, and then I was him—"

Lizzie noticed Lanny giving her one of those looks that only he and Matt understood.

"Hey, you're right, Lanny," Lizzie found

herself saying. "I could've hit my head on something."

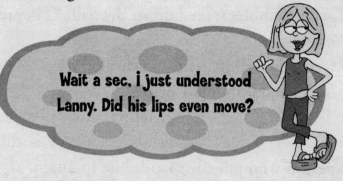

Wait a sec, i just understood Lanny. Did his lips even move?

"I miss my life!" wailed Lizzie. "My friends! My *shoes*!"

Lanny, Melina, and Lizzie all looked down at the shoes Lizzie had placed on Matt's feet that morning. They were penny loafers—nice, *shiny* penny loafers. And Lizzie had actually stuck pennies in them.

Suddenly, Lizzie blurted out, "Do you see what I see?"

"Yeah," said Melina, still looking at Matt's feet. "Totally dorky shoes."

"No," said Lizzie. "Those footprints." She pointed at the floor. Footprints made of gooey bubbles trailed down the hall. "They're *soapy*!"

Lanny nodded enthusiastically. Clearly, *he* understood, thought Lizzie.

"Oh, I get it," Melina finally said. "Whoever those footprints belong to is the person who put the soap in the fountain."

"And when we find that person," said Lizzie, "my little brother will be detention free."

Lanny put his hand on Matt's shoulder sympathetically. Lizzie appreciated it.

Then all three began to follow the footprints down the hall.

Back at Hillridge, Matt was finishing up his lunch period with Ethan Craft, Larry Tudgeman, Gordo, and Miranda.

Everyone was sitting around a table in the outdoor quad, totally fascinated by the amazingly cool stories that were pouring from Lizzie's mouth—courtesy of Matt McGuire!

". . . I've never had my stomach pumped before," Matt said, "but my friend Lanny has, and he said that . . ."

Gordo caught Miranda's eye and mouthed "Lanny?" Miranda just shrugged.

Suddenly, they were interrupted by the screech of an enraged voice.

"Lizzie McGuire!" cried Kate Sanders.

Kate stormed across the quad lawn, her hair and sweater dripping with chili.

"You rang?" said Matt.

"You owe me an apology!" Kate demanded.

Matt couldn't tell if her face was red with rage or chili sauce. Probably both, he figured.

"Oh, I'm sorry that you ran into a big bucket full of chili," said Matt.

Everyone at the table laughed.

Kate became even more furious. She turned to the others at the table. "That is not funny! Do you know what she did to me?"

Gordo lifted an eyebrow. "I'm guessing it had to do with *a bucket of chili*?"

"And banana peels!" cried Kate. "And frogs in my locker—"

"Frogs?" exclaimed Larry Tudgeman. "Wait, was *Murray* one of them? Oh, man, he was missing from the science lab." Larry jumped up from the table and started running toward the school building. "Which way? Which way? Murray, I'm coming for you, buddy!"

"Kate, Kate, Kate," said Ethan, shaking his head. "Lizzie didn't do any of that stuff."

"Yes, she did!" insisted Kate.

"Kate," said Matt, sweetening his "innocent" Lizzie voice off the sugar-shock chart. "I think you have me confused with someone else."

"Exactly," said Ethan. "I mean, *Lizzie* couldn't have done any of that stuff. I mean, it's . . . *Lizzie*."

Miranda nodded. "You know, Kate, he's right."

"And personally, I'm insulted," said Matt, impersonating a pained look he'd often seen on Lizzie's face. "You've besmirched my character, and I don't need to take that."

Matt rose from the table. "So, guys," he said sweetly, "thanks, it's been real. But I'm *outie*."

Matt couldn't stop himself from putting little finger quotes around "outie." It really wasn't something *he'd* ever say, but he knew the girlish slang was something Lizzie's friends would expect.

As he left, he brushed by Kate. *"Ribbit!"* he rasped, just to make her crazy.

Then, he called, "Later!" and headed inside.

Kate was in shock that nobody believed her. She sank down into Lizzie's seat at the table—and instantly jumped back up again.

"Lizzie!" she shrieked.

Everyone stared as Kate slowly turned around. An open peanut-butter-and-jelly sandwich had been left right there on Lizzie's seat.

And now it was stuck to *Kate's*!

Meanwhile, over at the elementary school, Lizzie, Lanny, and Melina were still following the soapy footprint trail.

When it finally ended, they looked up. Their suspect was standing right in front of them.

That nerdy-looking boy from lunch, Clark Benson, saw the three approaching and quickly tried to shut his locker door and rush away. But Melina's hand blocked him.

"Not so fast, Clark Benson," said Melina.

"I didn't do it!" Clark cried.

"Then how do you know we're accusing you of something?" Lizzie asked.

"Okay, fine, I admit it," said Clark. "The only reason I put soap in the fountain was so that you'd stop sneezing in my pudding! It's disgusting . . . and I *like* my pudding!"

The kid's got a point.

"You know what?" Lizzie told Clark. "You're right. That *is* disgusting. And I'm totally sorry, and it won't happen again."

Melina frowned. If she had any doubt at all before, she now knew *very* well that Matt wasn't inside his own body. She turned to

Lizzie. "I don't think you're *authorized* to make that kind of promise," she said.

Lizzie narrowed her eyes at Melina. "*Yes*, I am."

Clark studied Matt, wondering whether to believe him. Then he looked at Lanny and Melina. They both just shrugged.

"*Really?*" Clark asked Matt.

"Really," Lizzie said in a firm Matt voice. "In fact, for the rest of the week . . . no, for the rest of the year . . . I *promise* I won't sneeze in your pudding ever again."

"In that case," said Clark, "I'll tell Principal Alder that I'm the one who put the bubbles in the fountain."

Great. No detention! But will i be stuck this way forever?!

CHAPTER SIX

After the school day finally ended, Matt strutted into the McGuires' living room. The whole day had passed and nothing had changed. He was still stuck in his big sister's body. And she was still stuck in *his*, he discovered as he walked into the room and found her sitting on the couch, doing homework. *Homework!* He *never* did homework this early, if he even did it at all! What would people think if they saw him . . . er . . . HER?

They'd think he'd turned into a big goody-goody!

Lizzie looked up from Matt's schoolwork.

"Well?" she asked as she jumped off the couch. "How'd it go? Could anybody tell? What happened today?"

"Nothing," said Matt. "What happened with you?"

"Okay," said Lizzie, annoyed. "I'm not Mom and Dad, Matt. 'Nothing' *didn't* happen today. Now tell me everything, you little weasel!"

Lizzie tugged Matt down beside her on the couch.

"You know," Matt told his sister, "that's really the attitude that you should have at school. If you treated Kate the way that you treated me, then you'd be set."

"Why?" asked Lizzie, still worried. "What happened?"

"Let's just say that things got a little 'chili' at school today." Matt grinned. "So what happened with you?"

"Well, you got three weeks' detention for doing something you didn't do," Lizzie told him.

"Three weeks!" cried Matt. Then he shrugged. "It happens."

"Not to *my* little brother. I tracked down the guy who deserved it, Clark Benson. *But* you've got to stop sneezing in his pudding."

"Me?" said Matt, dragging out the innocent act for the umpteenth time. "Sneezing in his pudding? Well, that's disgusting."

"Hey," called Mrs. McGuire, passing by with a laundry basket. "What happened at school today?"

"Nothing," said Lizzie.

"Nothing," echoed Matt.

"Okay," said Mrs. McGuire with a shrug.

"Dinner'll be ready soon. Don't forget to wash up."

After Mrs. McGuire left the room, Lizzie turned to her brother. "Do you think we'll be stuck like this forever?"

Matt collapsed on the seat of the couch. "Man, I hope not."

"Me, too," said Lizzie, collapsing with him.

Make that *three* of us.

That night, Lizzie tossed and turned. Matt's bed was all lumpy. And it *smelled*! And his stupid "sports hero" sheets felt scratchy.

And to top off the worst *day* of my life, the worst *night* of my life! i miss my bed!

Suddenly, Matt's body rolled completely off the bed and onto the floor with a loud *thump.*

"Ow!" Matt said as his eyes snapped open.

Next door, in Lizzie's bed, Lizzie's body bolted upright.

Lizzie looked around. Wait a second, she thought. Something was different . . . or more like *familiar*!

She noticed some hair hanging in front of her face—*long, blond* hair!

She raced to the mirror and saw *herself* there!

Finally, finally, finally! she thought.

"I'm . . . I'm me again!" she cried.

Whoo-hoo! i'M BACK!
Oh, i missed me so much!

"Matt!" Lizzie called as she raced out of her bedroom and into the hall.

Matt heard her calling and met her there. "What?" he asked.

Like a long-lost bud, Lizzie hugged her brother tightly. "We switched back again!" she cried.

Matt squinted at her. "Why are you *hugging* me?"

Down the hall, another bedroom door opened. Mr. McGuire and Mrs. McGuire appeared, scratching their sleepy heads.

"Kids," said Mr. McGuire with a yawn, "it's the middle of the night."

"What are you guys doing?" asked Mrs. McGuire, confused. Then she realized her children had been hugging. Hugging?!

"Were you guys actually *talking* and *not* fighting?" asked Mrs. McGuire, in shock. She put her hand to her heart. "I *must* be dreaming."

Lizzie and Matt shared a look. The sort of look that said, "We have a secret you'll *never* guess."

But Lizzie knew her mother was waiting for some sort of explanation. "We forgot to say good night to each other," Lizzie told her.

"That's all," Matt quickly agreed.

"Good night," Lizzie said.

"Sweet dreams," Matt sang.

As Mr. McGuire and Mrs. McGuire shuffled back into their room, Mr. McGuire muttered, "Maybe we *are* dreaming." Then he pinched Mrs. McGuire to check.

"Hey!" she complained and swatted her husband in the stomach.

"Ow!" said Mr. McGuire. "Guess not."

After their parents shut their bedroom door, Lizzie turned to Matt. "So, do you think that really happened?"

"Do I think *what* really happened?" asked Matt.

if he's not saying, then neither am i.

"Good night, Matt," said Lizzie. "Sweet dreams."

"'Night," said Matt.

Then Matt and Lizzie went back to their

own rooms and their *own* beds. Whether she had imagined the whole switcheroo thing or not, Lizzie was happy that she was back in her own body. And though she wasn't about to let her brother borrow anything of hers anytime in the near future (especially her personality!), she suddenly had a new, and *way* unique, perspective on the kid. Maybe he wasn't *always* as bad as he seemed.

Though she hated to admit it, it *was* kind of fun being Matt for a day. Even so, she had missed being herself. And she, for one, was glad that Lizzie McGuire—the *real* Lizzie McGuire—was back . . . now and forever!

PART TWO

CHAPTER ONE

Lizzie rolled her eyes in disgust as she walked into the kitchen. Once again, the little freak claiming to be her brother was acting like a total weirdo.

For the past hour, he'd been holding his annual trick-or-treat "strategy session" with his friend, Lanny.

"Okay, here's our Halloween battle plan," Matt announced, hunched over a street map at the kitchen table.

"The houses marked in red give out the

best candies," explained Matt. "The houses in blue give out little boxes of raisins—we'll blow them off."

Lanny nodded in agreement.

"Then we take the D bus to Rancho Vista Estates," Matt continued. "They're all rich, and they give out *full*-size candy bars and dollar bills."

Lanny drummed the table with enthusiasm.

Yanking open the refrigerator door, Lizzie sighed. How greedy can a boy get? she thought.

"You know what you should go as, Matt?" she asked as she grabbed a bottle of sparkling water. "A troll. That way you wouldn't need makeup."

"Actually, I *was* gonna be the Ugliest Kid on Earth, but *you're* already wearing the costume," jeered Matt.

Lanny thrust his arms in the air, giving

Matt a double high five for that one.
Lizzie seethed.

This is it—Matt is going down.
Aw, crud! Here come Mom and Dad.

Matt looked up at his mother with innocent eyes. "Hey, Mom," he said sweetly, "my Halloween trick-or-treat bag was too small last year. Can I borrow the wheelbarrow?"

"Uh, champ," said Mr. McGuire, "you're not going to need a trick-or-treat bag this year, 'cause you're not going trick-or-treatin'."

Matt looked too stunned to speak—which totally amused Lizzie. *Motormouth* stunned speechless? "Ha-ha!" she cackled. "You're busted, little brother!"

"Now, don't worry," Mrs. McGuire quickly told Matt in a soothing voice. "You're going to have a good time. You're going to go to the Halloween Fright Night at your sister's school."

"He's—*what*?!" cried Lizzie. *Dweeb-boy* was coming to her school? Having *live* vampires come to Hillridge was a less frightening thought.

"Ha-ha!" Matt taunted right back. Lanny pointed at Lizzie and silently laughed, too.

"Look," said Mr. McGuire, pulling out a flyer. "They've got haunted dungeons, game booths, prizes, everything. . . ."

"Hello?!" cried Lizzie. "Nobody asked *me* about this. If stink-boy comes to my Fright Night, I'm gonna have a terrible time!"

"Aw, you will?" said Matt, faking a frown. Then he shouted with glee, "I'm there!"

Great. i get to brat-sit my little brother. Talk about *scary*. Trick-or-treat. . . .

CHAPTER TWO

At school a week later, Lizzie filed into an empty classroom with her best friend, Miranda, and a bunch of student volunteers.

The planning meeting for the annual Hillridge Junior High Fright Night was officially underway. And Lizzie wanted to scream.

It wasn't the ghosts and jack-o'-lanterns drawn on the chalkboard that scared her. It was the *thing* that stood in front of them.

Kate Sanders, queen of the cheer-beasts, was this year's head of the Fright Night party committee. In all her glory, she addressed the room in her typical "I'm all that" mode: perfect hair, perfect makeup, clipboard held in her French-manicured hands. A scary sight, for sure. And there was nothing Lizzie could do about it.

"So the girls' soccer team will be in charge of painting the soccer balls like human heads for the 'Guess How Many Human Heads Are in the Barrel of Heads' game," Kate smugly announced.

Larry Tudgeman waved his hand in the air. "Oh! Oh! Oh!"

"*What*, Tudgeman?" Kate asked with a sneer. Being forced to actually *talk* to such a lowly geek obviously pained her.

Wearing his usual putty-colored shirt with its lime green collar, Larry leaped to his feet.

Then he cleared his throat dramatically and said, "Luke, I am your father."

Everyone stared.

"That's Darth Vader," Larry explained excitedly. "I do a *great* Darth Vader. I could scare people with that."

"Sit down, Tudgeman," said Kate, not bothering to hide her disgust. "Okay, let's discuss decorations."

Miranda stood right up. She had a great idea and couldn't wait to share it. "I want to display skeleton dolls from El Día de los Muertos, which is the Day of the Dead, which is Halloween in Mexico," she explained.

Kate shook her head and waved Miranda away. "Why would we want to display your stuff?"

"'Cause it's cool," said Miranda.

"No, it's not," said Kate. "It's *lame*."

Lizzie wanted to smack Kate. Miranda actually looked hurt.

In a loud voice, Lizzie immediately defended her bud. "I think it's *great* to have stuff from other countries at our party."

"Yeah!" agreed Miranda.

The other kids in the room seemed to think so, too. They began to nod, and a bunch of them joined Miranda in shouting, *Yeah!*

Lizzie grinned. Kate *totally* lost this round, and there was nothing she could do about it.

"Fine," Kate snapped at Miranda. "You can have your stupid little toys set up on a table."

"They're miniature skeletons that represent dead ancestors, so you'd better treat them well," warned Miranda.

Tudgeman leaped to his feet again. "Treat them well you must," he said in a high, squeaky voice. "Wise they are, yes."

The room of kids stared at Tudgeman again. *Huh?*

"That's Yoda," he explained.

Lizzie hated to burst the Tudge's bubble, but he just wasn't helping. "Tudgeman—" Lizzie began.

"I know," he said. "Sit down and zip it?"

Lizzie nodded.

Miranda narrowed her eyes at Kate. "I mean it," she continued. "A kid in Veracruz made fun of the spirits once. And after three days, he was found in a coffin, surrounded by skeletons. His hair turned white, and he never, ever, ever spoke again."

Miranda's story actually freaked out some of the kids. They gave one another uneasy looks.

"All right," Kate said dismissively, "we'll treat them well. Anything else?"

Lizzie gathered her courage and rose to her

feet. Miranda had taken a chance and got her idea accepted, thought Lizzie. So why not me, too?

"I'd like to sign up to be Vampire Mistress in the Dungeon of Terror," said Lizzie hopefully.

i would look so slinky and cool as a vampire. i am so tired of wearing Mom's old marching band uniform every year.

"You should let her, Kate," said Miranda quickly. "Lizzie would be really good."

Lizzie slipped Miranda a *"Thanks, bud"* look.

"Well . . ." said Kate, making a sour face as

she thought about it. "I *guess* I could let you be the Dungeon Mistress."

"Really?" Lizzie said. *Wow!* she thought. Could Kate's heart of rock-solid ice actually be melting?

"Yeah," said Kate, "but you're going to have to clean out the janitor's utility room where we're putting the dungeon."

"Oh," said Lizzie. So much for melting the ice queen's heart. "It's yucky in there."

"Hey," called Tudgeman, refusing to give up his George Lucas dreams. "I do a great Wookie—" He started bellowing like Chewbacca.

Unfortunately, impersonating the lion-ape roar of the *Star Wars* alien took its toll on Tudgeman's vocal cords. After a few seconds, he doubled over in a fit of coughing and choking.

No one acted concerned—although Tudgeman didn't seem to notice.

"It's okay," he said between hacking coughs. "I'm solid."

Later that afternoon, Lizzie made her way over to the janitor's closet. The musty space was packed with filthy old mops, mildewed cardboard cartons, leaky pipes, moldy rags, rusty buckets, and bags of trash.

"Ew . . ." Lizzie grimaced. "It's even grosser than I thought."

"Of course, it's gross," said Lizzie's other best friend, Gordo, beside her. "It's where the janitor keeps his bucket of throw-up sand."

Excuse me? thought Lizzie, shooting a disturbed look at Gordo.

"For whenever a kid around here throws up," he explained. "That's it right there."

Lizzie shuddered at the crud-crusted bucket. "I swear, Kate Sanders spends, like, all of her time just thinking of ways to make me miserable," she said.

"I don't think that's true," said Gordo. "I think Kate Sanders spends all of her time thinking of ways to make *everybody* miserable."

"Well, it'll be worth it to be a vampire hottie," said Lizzie. "Thanks for helping me, Gordo."

Gordo glared at Lizzie as if she'd just lost her mind. "I'm not helping you!" he said. "You just said to meet you here. You said you were gonna give me a hamburger."

"But you *have* to help me," Lizzie pleaded. The place was way too creepy to clean all by herself, she thought—and Miranda had flat-out refused.

"Why would I help you?" argued Gordo. "So you can once again do exactly what Kate Sanders wants? So you can let her manipulate you and every other kid in this school who hopes and prays for their fifteen minutes of popularity? Why on earth would I *participate* in that?"

Lizzie smiled slyly. "Because my cousin Heather's coming into town again next summer and I'm gonna get her to go out with you."

Gordo's eyes widened. "Quit your yappin'," he cried, lunging for the cluttered shelves. "We've got work to do!"

Over the next two hours, Lizzie and Gordo carried out boxes of supplies, dragged out trash bags, mopped the dirty floor, scrubbed the moldy sink, and battled a roach the size of a pickup truck.

By the time they were done, the closet looked as clean as a hospital ward. Gordo and Lizzie, however, looked as though they'd crawled out of a sewer.

This is gross, thought Lizzie, through it all. But it's worth it. Hottie vampire costume, here I come!

As Gordo headed for the boys' room to clean up, Lizzie trudged through the school halls in search of Kate.

Lizzie's face was dirty, her clothes were soiled, and her hair was grungy, but she didn't even care that kids were giving her curious looks as she passed them in the hall. All she could think about was how *cool* she was going to look on Fright Night!

Maybe Ethan Craft will *actually, finally* notice me, thought Lizzie—along with some of those cute boys on the football team. This could be a whole new image for me!

When she found Kate, she strode right up to her and announced, "The utility room is all clean, Kate."

"What a good little cleaner you are," said

Kate, patting Lizzie on the head like she was a preschooler.

Holding her temper, Lizzie just said, "I'll need props for the dungeon, so I can start decorating it."

"Oh, I forgot to tell you," said Kate. "*I* decided to be the Vampira dungeon mistress. I need *you* to be Floppy the Clown and give out balloons."

"What?!" cried Lizzie. "You said if I cleaned out that slop hole, I could be Vampira!"

"I know," said Kate, "but as head of the party committee, I decided that Vampira should be someone tall and desirable." She splayed her French-manicured fingers across her chest. "And that's me."

I should have *known* Kate would pull a stunt like this! thought Lizzie. She wanted to tell Kate exactly what she should do with her Floppy the Clown balloons, but before she could even utter a word, Kate sang, "See ya'," then turned on her heel, whipped her long blond hair in Lizzie's face, and left.

NO! *i* am the desirable vampire! *i* get to wear the slinky outfit! *i* get to—oh, okay, i'm gonna need about eight gallons of concealer for this stupid clown nose!

CHAPTER THREE

A few days later, Halloween had finally arrived! Matt was sitting with his mom in their kitchen. "I need some gross stuff for my costume," he told her. "I'm going as me, turned inside out."

"I know, I know," said Mrs. McGuire, who'd been hearing about Matt's many possible Halloween costumes since Labor Day.

A few nights ago, Matt had finally made his decision. Wearing bones and fake bloody guts had won out over pretending to be either a roll of toilet paper, or a *cereal* killer—which would have involved carrying around a box of cornflakes and a rubber knife.

"Oh," said Matt, peering into the open fridge. "Can I use this spaghetti sauce?"

"No, honey," Mrs. McGuire said sweetly. "That's for dinner tomorrow night."

"How 'bout this caviar stuff?" asked Matt. "It looks like brains."

"You may not use the caviar," said Mrs. McGuire. "That's for your father and me tonight."

Matt sighed. He pushed a jar of pickles aside and peered farther into the fridge. "How about those sausages?"

"Oh, I suppose," said Mrs. McGuire. "Sure."

Matt excitedly reached for the bowl. He lifted a few cold, slimy links. "Oh, gross," he said. Then he held them up to his stomach as he walked out of the kitchen. "Ahh, my guts are falling out!"

All the while, Mr. McGuire was carving a pumpkin at the kitchen table. "You got caviar for us tonight?" he asked, walking over to his wife.

"Yeah," said Mrs. McGuire. "The trick-or-treaters are gonna probably be done by seven-thirty, and then we're gonna have the house to ourselves."

"No kids?" asked Mr. McGuire.

"No screaming," said Mrs. McGuire.

"Nobody fighting over the TV remote?" asked Mr. McGuire.

"Just you and me," said Mrs. McGuire.

"Yeah!" Mr. McGuire gave his wife a big kiss, just as Matt came back into the kitchen, wearing part of his inside-out costume.

With his bloody eyeballs hanging out of their sockets, Matt looked at his parents kissing and cried, "Gross! That is so disgusting!"

Mr. McGuire glanced at his son. "Look who's talkin'."

Meanwhile, over at Hillridge Junior High, the Fright Night party committee was hard at work decorating the cafeteria.

Orange and black streamers hung from the ceiling. Homemade ghosts, skeletons, and black cats lined the walls. And big jack-o'-lanterns were set out everywhere.

Kate stood in the middle of the room, directing the flurry of activity.

Nearby, Miranda snapped some batteries into a plastic skull, then called, "Hey, Kate."

When Kate glanced over, Miranda clapped her hands. The skull's eyes flashed red, and it gave off a startling graveyard cackle.

Kate flinched in surprise, and Miranda laughed.

"Oh, real *mature*," sneered Kate.

Miranda rolled her eyes. "Oh, yes, it's *very* immature of us to play with toy skulls on Halloween," she said sarcastically. "We'll *try* to grow up."

Just then, Miranda's mother walked in, carrying a cardboard box and a shopping bag.

"Did somebody order a box of skulls?" she asked cheerfully.

"Hey, Mom," said Miranda. "Where's Dad?"

"Oh, he's coming," said Mrs. Sanchez. "He had a little *accident* in the parking lot."

That was apparently the "cue" for Miranda's father to walk in. He waved around the right sleeve of his raincoat wildly. At the end of it, there appeared to be nothing but a bloody stump.

"I may need a needle and thread," he told Miranda. "I got my sleeve caught in the car door." He was holding a rubber right hand in his "remaining" left one.

"Careful, Dad," said Miranda, laughing. "Kate will tell you you're immature."

"Oh, Miranda, I *love* your parents. They know that!" declared Kate with the same fake sincerity she used on teachers the week before final exams. "Hi, Mrs. Sanchez. How *are* you, Mr. Sanchez?"

Miranda's mother showed Kate the box and bag of Mexican skeleton dolls.

"Oh, how interesting," said Kate through gritted teeth.

"Day of the Dead is one of my favorite holidays," said Mr. Sanchez as he and his wife began unpacking things. They placed a pair of two-foot-high skeletons on the refreshments table. The skeletons were dressed in wedding clothes.

Then Mrs. Sanchez pulled a dinner plate

out of the bag and put it on the table next to the skeleton bride and groom.

"Yeah," she said. "And on El Día de los Muertos, in Mexico, people go to the cemetery and have a meal with the dead."

Kate's fake smile finally fell at that. She stared at Miranda's mother in horror.

"It's a lot more fun than it sounds," said Mrs. Sanchez. "There's dances and all kinds of stuff."

"The tamale represents the meal," said Mr. Sanchez, placing the tamale on the plate in front of the skeletons. "It's chicken," he said. "The dead have to watch their cholesterol."

Kate chuckled at the joke—but the laugh was far from genuine, and her eyes narrowed into little, irritated slits. "Thank you *so* much for sharing this with us," she said in a totally fake cheery tone. "It is going to make our Fright Night *so* much more interesting."

"Well, it's our pleasure," said Mrs. Sanchez. Then she pinched Miranda's cheek and added, "And now I think we're gonna get out of here so you kids can finish decorating."

"Thanks, Mom. Thanks, Dad," said Miranda.

Mr. Sanchez smiled as he handed Kate his "severed" right hand. "Here, Kate. Give Miranda a 'hand' with the rest of this stuff."

Kate dangled the rubber hand by a finger, barely hiding her disgust.

"Come on," said Mrs. Sanchez. Then she and her husband headed for the door.

"Oh, hi, Mr. and Mrs. Sanchez," said Lizzie as she walked in.

"We're just on our way out," said Miranda's dad.

"We'll see you later, Lizzie," Miranda's mom added.

"Thanks again, Mr. and Mrs. Sanchez! We

really appreciate it!" Kate called in her sickly sweet voice.

But the second Miranda's parents were gone, Kate's supersweet voice soured into a superharsh snarl. "Get that stupid junk off the refreshment table!"

Do you believe Kate? She's phonier than cafeteria cheese.

Kate snatched up the bride and groom skeletons and shoved them into Miranda's arms. "Take your little ancestors and stick them in the corner," she commanded.

Miranda was about to protest, but Kate cut her off.

"*I'm* in charge here," said Kate. "*I* say where stuff goes."

"You know what, Kate?" said Miranda. "I don't care what you do to me. But you should *so* not dis my dead ancestors. If you get 'em mad, *bad stuff* can happen."

"Oooh, I'm so scared," said Kate, rolling her eyes.

Miranda and Lizzie shared a disgusted look, then carried the skeletons over to a small table in the corner of the room, below a big window.

"Kate shouldn't come as a vampire," complained Miranda. "She should come as a sewer rat."

"So, do these things really have powers?" Lizzie asked hopefully. She picked up the skeleton groom.

"Go get Kate. Sic her, boy," Lizzie told the skeleton, jokingly. "Go get her. I'll give you a bone!"

Lizzie put the skeleton down again. "I guess

they don't really work. Too bad. It'd be cool if they did, though."

A roll of thunder sounded as Lizzie and Miranda left the skeletons and rejoined the crew of kids decorating the room. Neither of them noticed the bright bolt of lightning that flashed through the window—or how it made the skeletons' eyes seem to come alive.

CHAPTER FOUR

A few hours later, Hilldridge Junior High's annual Fright Night was in full swing.

The cafeteria was packed with kids in costumes, playing games and dancing to the rockin' tunes of a student deejay.

About the only person *not* having fun was Lizzie. She felt like a total frump loser in her baggy clown costume, complete with a stupid top hat and a *really* stupid red clown nose.

But that wasn't the worst part. The worst

part was her official Floppy the Clown job for Fright Night—making "balloon animals" for all the kids.

Lizzie didn't have a clue how to make a balloon animal. The one or two times she tried to twist a few of the long, tubular balloons into some sort of dog or giraffe shape, they popped in her hands. So she gave up.

"Here," she said, finally shoving a balloon tube at one kid. "It's a snake."

"Here," she said, handing out another. "It's a worm."

"Here," she said on the third. "It's, uh . . . spaghetti."

This is brutal, thought Lizzie. I can't be expected to come up with tube-shaped names all night!

The next kid in line was her brother, Matt. His inside-out costume looked really gross. Fake bones, blood, and guts were plastered all over a red-splattered bodysuit. He wore a "cranium and brain matter" cap on his head, and a pair of glasses that were covered in fake scar flesh and made it look like his slimy eyeballs were hanging out.

"Here," said Lizzie, slapping the long, thin tube into his hand. "It's a caterpillar."

"This is a lame balloon animal," complained Matt.

"Oh, sorry. Let me fix it," said Lizzie. Then she reached out and popped the balloon with her fingernail.

"Oh!" she said. "There, now it's *extinct*."

Shaking her head, Lizzie put down the rest of her balloons.

Time to visit Miranda at her booth, she thought, *if* I can manage to get over there without tripping over my stupid Floppy the Clown feet!

* * *

At Miranda's "Smashing Pumpkins" booth, Gordo was ecstatic. "Yeah, I did it!" he shouted.

With one toss of the softball, he'd managed to knock down all the stuffed pumpkins.

Inside the booth, Miranda clapped her Cat in the Hat paws. "Hey! You win one coupon!" she said, handing him a ticket.

"How many do I need to get the lava lamp?" asked Gordo.

"Three hundred and seven," said Miranda, twitching her hand-drawn whiskers and little black cat nose.

Gordo sighed. "Well, what can I get with one?"

Miranda held up the choices. "A hair scrunchie or a Burger Buddy."

Gordo shrugged. "Then I guess gimme the Burger Buddy."

Burger Buddy was just a stupid plastic

bobble-headed toy from a fast-food chain. But Gordo figured it was better than a girlie hair scrunchie.

Just then, Lizzie walked up. "Can you guys believe Kate?" she said, totally annoyed.

Lizzie gestured to the refreshments table nearby. Kate was standing next to it, sipping punch—and *dressed as the Vampire Mistress*! The slinky black costume, red lipstick, dark eyeliner, and cloud of teased blond hair made Kate look really hot. So, of course, one of the cutest guys on the football team was talking to her—and obviously going gaga over the outfit.

No surprise, Lizzie thought as she sneered over at Kate.

Gordo turned his head. For the first time, he had caught a look at Kate's costume.

"Holy ravioli!" he cried.

Gordo's eyes bugged out so far, he looked

like he'd swiped Matt's hanging eyeballs—which would have been totally wrong for the theme of his costume, thought Lizzie.

This year, Gordo had dressed as something he called Guy Caught in a Windstorm. His tie was starched so it stuck out behind him, his jacket appeared blown open, and his hair was gelled so it stood straight up. The whole effect was subtle, yet witty—in other words, typical Gordo.

Of course, after Lizzie saw his bug-eyed reaction to Kate's costume, she was ready to send him out into a *real* windstorm—preferably *hurricane* level.

"I *mean*, can you believe how she just stole my costume?" Lizzie snapped.

"Oh. Right. Yeah," said Gordo, recovering. "Terrible thing to do."

"Man, this is a good tamale," said Matt, walking up to Lizzie, Gordo, and Miranda.

He set down his cup of lemonade on a nearby table and added, "Got any more of 'em?"

Miranda's jaw nearly hit the floor. She pointed at the half-eaten tamale in Matt's hand. "Where did you get that?"

"Over there, where the skeletons are getting married," Matt said.

Miranda looked like she was about to faint. "You *ate* the food offering of the Day of the Dead?! You *stole* the sacred meal of my *dead ancestors*?!"

"It had cheese on it," Matt said with a shrug.

"Do you know what you've done? You have offended the spirits," said Miranda, her loud voice attracting the attention of Kate, who was still standing at the nearby refreshments table.

"You have opened the door to this world and the next," Miranda continued. "You have unleashed the dark, angry forces of the restless dead!"

Lizzie stared at her brother. "Way to go, beef-head."

"All right, let's not get carried away here," said Gordo in his Mr. Calm tone. "Day of the Dead's a holiday just like any other holiday. Matt, all you did was eat a tamale—you didn't wake up any supernatural forces."

"Good," said Matt with relief. Then he reached for his lemonade to wash down the rest of the tamale.

"Whoa! Hey!" he cried, alarmed. "What happened to my lemonade? It . . . it turned black!"

"What's that?" asked Kate, walking over. She pointed at Matt's punch cup. It was full of bubbling dark liquid.

"*That* was lemonade?" Gordo asked.

"It *was*. Now it smells all moldy and rotten and . . . dead," said Matt.

Lizzie looked at the Day of the Dead table. She squinted in disbelief.

"Kate," called Lizzie, "did you move the bride and groom skeletons?"

"No," said Kate. She peered across the room at the table where Miranda's two-foot-tall skeletons had been sitting. All the decorations were still there, including the plate for the food offering Matt had just scoffed down. But the skeletons were missing.

"Miranda, did you move them?" asked Lizzie.

"No," said Miranda.

Suddenly, Matt screamed. "What's that?!"

He pointed across the room, where two life-size bride and groom skeletons were just disappearing out the cafeteria doors!

"The spirits are awake," whispered Miranda. "Evil and doom walk the night."

CHAPTER FIVE

Twenty minutes later, Kate Sanders was still freaking out.

"There must be an innocent explanation for all this," Gordo told her.

The two of them were standing in front of the Day of the Dead table, staring at the empty spaces where the bride and groom skeletons had been sitting.

"Then explain why the lemonade was black," said Kate, still upset.

"It's *cafeteria* lemonade," said Gordo, trying to talk some sense into her. "You know what the food's like around here—it's mostly bacteria. You let the beef stew sit out for two minutes, and it grows legs and hops away."

"Well, I don't want anything ruining my party," said Kate, turning away from the table and walking back toward the refreshments area. "We'll replace the lemonade with fruit punch."

Just then, both Kate and Gordo noticed Lizzie rushing across the floor to Miranda.

"Miranda!" cried Lizzie. "Uh. I'm a little freaked out. This whole Day of the Dead stuff is just superstition, right? I mean, someone probably just moved those skeletons."

"Right. Right . . . it's probably just superstition," said Miranda hesitantly.

"Good," said Lizzie. "Because Tudgeman told me that Matt disappeared. They were, like, showing each other how to dislocate their jaws, and, all of a sudden, there was a flash of light, and this dust."

Lizzie held up a plastic cup full of dust, and Miranda looked horrified.

"La loda de los muertos!" she said pointing at the cup, her eyes wide. "The mud of the Dead. My grandmother used to talk about what would happen if you made the spirits angry. Matt ate their tamale; now they've taken revenge."

Kate gasped. And Gordo rushed over to Lizzie and Miranda.

"This is ridiculous," he told them, but his voice sounded worried—and a little bit scared. "No skeletons got up and walked away. There are no spirits taking revenge."

"Well, look what they did to Matt," said Lizzie, holding up the cup in her hand.

"That's not Matt. That's dirt," said Gordo.

"If it's dirt, then why is one of his eyeballs in it?" asked Lizzie. She plunged two fingers into the cup and pulled out one of the fake hanging eyeballs from Matt's costume.

"He's probably in the bathroom or playing in the gym," said Gordo quickly. "And you guys are getting hysterical about ghosts and goblins, and it's ridiculous."

Then Gordo turned his face to the heavens. "Do you hear me? I think it's stupid! Come on, spirits, turn me into dust!"

For a few seconds, Lizzie, Miranda, and Kate held their breath.

"See? Nothing," said Gordo with a shrug.

"Nothing *yet*," said Miranda.

As they continued to argue over what had happened to Matt, none of them noticed the life-size bride and groom skeletons peeking into the cafeteria doorway, then slipping away. . . .

The truth is, if Matt *did* get spirited away to the realm of the dead, who's gonna be in trouble with Mom and Dad? *Me!*

While Lizzie was freaking out at Fright Night, her parents were just about to close the door on another season's trick-or-treaters.

Mrs. McGuire settled into the living room couch. Romantic candles lit the room, and a cozy meal for two was waiting on the coffee table.

"Sam, come on," Mrs. McGuire called to her husband. "Your food's going to get cold."

At the front door, Mr. McGuire gave one last look up and down the dark street. The crowds of kids had come and gone, and the neighborhood looked quiet again.

"Well, there's no more trick-or-treaters," he

called to his wife. Then he checked his watch. "It's eight o'clock. Pumpkin's coming in. Porch light goes off. I'm calling it a night."

He carried the glowing jack-o'-lantern into the living room with him.

Mrs. McGuire patted the couch cushion next to her and smiled.

"Now that's a treat," said Mr. McGuire, looking at the nice hot dinner that was waiting for him.

He was about to sit down when the doorbell rang. Mr. McGuire sighed. Another trick-or-treater?

"Be right back," he said, dropping the jack-o'-lantern on the cushion next to his wife. Mrs. McGuire glanced unhappily at the jack-o'-lantern. She'd wanted to be sitting next to her husband, not a carved pumpkin!

When Mr. McGuire opened the door, he found a big, and *familiar*, teenager standing there, wearing jeans, a T-shirt splattered with fake blood, and one of those rubber knives that made it look as if a blade were pierced through his head.

"Trick or treat," barked the kid with a grimace.

"Hey, you were just here fifteen minutes ago," said Mr. McGuire.

"Uh. No, I wasn't," said the kid. "Now, gimme some candy."

"Yeah, you *were*. I gave you our last candy bar," said Mr. McGuire, annoyed with the kid's nasty attitude.

"Wasn't me. Now, hand over the candy," the kid demanded.

"Yeah, it *was* you," said Mr. McGuire. "You think I wouldn't remember this costume? Who are you supposed to be, anyway?"

"Um, I'm the knife guy," said the kid. "Now, gimme some candy, old man. Ticktock."

Inside the house, Mrs. McGuire was getting impatient. Hearing the argument, she left the pumpkin head on the couch and walked to the front door, still holding her dinner plate.

"Sam, just give him some candy and get rid of him," she said.

"I don't have more candy," he told her.

"Here," said Mrs. McGuire, shoving her dinner plate into the kid's hands. "Have some chicken potpie."

"What?" cried the kid, caught off guard. He stared down at the plate.

"No, it's good. Take it," said Mrs. McGuire waving him away.

"Chicken potpie? I'm a vegetarian," complained the kid.

But Mr. McGuire was done listening to the obnoxious kid. So he shut the door right in his face.

CHAPTER SIX

Back at Fright Night, Lizzie, Miranda, Gordo, and Kate all agreed to split up and look for Matt.

Gordo went to the boys' room, Lizzie went to the quad outside, and Kate and Miranda went to the gym.

Finding no one in the gym or the locker room, Kate strode back to the cafeteria. Miranda was right on her heels.

"You heard Gordo," Kate told Miranda as they pushed through the cafeteria's double doors. "This is just superstition. Until some-body proves it's not, I'm going to enjoy myself."

But the grin on Kate's face began to disap-pear when she heard the disembodied voice of Gordo calling, "Help! Lizzie? Miranda?! Help!"

"Gordo?" Kate called.

"Gordo? Where are you?" asked Miranda, looking around.

"I don't know! I can't see anything. What's going on?" asked the voice. It sounded like Gordo. But it was weirdly high and tinny.

"Gordo? What happened?" Miranda called into the air.

"I don't know. Help me!" cried the voice in a panic.

Suddenly, Kate and Miranda realized the voice was emanating from a fake gravestone near the refreshments table. On top of the gravestone sat the little ceramic Burger Buddy that Gordo had won earlier.

"Ohmigosh," said Miranda, creeping closer to the plastic toy. "You're *inside* the Burger Buddy."

"Ohmigosh, you're in the Burger Buddy," echoed Kate, alarmed.

"I am?" said Gordo's tinny voice. "Oh, well, get me out!"

"How?!" Kate asked, staring at the grinning bobbling head of the Burger Buddy.

"It's the spirits," said Miranda, eyes wide. "They did this."

"This is your fault," said Kate, freaking out on Miranda. "You had to bring those Day of the Dead things."

"Stop arguing," said Gordo. "Just get me out of here."

But Miranda wasn't listening. She was too busy reacting to Kate's accusation.

"Well, *you* shouldn't have dissed them," Miranda told Kate. Then she gave her a little shove.

"Tell the spirits I'm sorry," babbled Gordo. "Tell them I'm scared."

"Don't try to blame this on me!" said Kate, shoving Miranda right back.

Miranda stumbled into the gravestone, and the Burger Buddy was knocked off.

"Tell my parents I miss them," cried Gordo as the Burger Buddy plunged toward the floor. "I don't know if I'll ever—AAAGGHH!"

SMASH!

The Burger Buddy shattered into a dozen pieces. And Gordo's voice fell silent.

For a few seconds, Kate and Miranda just stared in shock at the shattered toy.

"Gordo?" rasped Miranda, close to tears. Then she pointed at Kate. "Look what you did!"

"I didn't do it!" cried Kate, totally freaking

now. "Don't try to blame this on me. You pushed me first!"

Across the room, sudden screams and shouts sounded. Floppy the Clown had burst through the kitchen doors, startling a group of kids.

With arms held stiffly in front of her, Lizzie walked forward, wearing her clown suit and a demented stare. Her eyes looked sunken with black rings around them, and her cheeks looked hollow, like a corpse's!

"KA-ATE . . ." Lizzie moaned.

"Lizzie? Are you okay?" called Miranda, uneasily.

Lizzie failed to respond to her best friend's voice. She just kept walking and moaning—as if she were completely zombified. Or totally insane!

"KA-ATE . . ." Lizzie moaned again, moving closer.

"Lizzie!" called Kate.

"Lizzie, cut it out," Miranda said, visibly shaken now. "You're *scaring* me."

As Lizzie passed a kid in a pirate costume, she grabbed a curved dagger from his belt. She waved it around—until she saw that it was just a rubber toy.

"RUB-BER . . . bad. . . ." groaned Lizzie, throwing the knife aside.

"She's turned into a zombie!" cried Kate. "I've seen this in movies."

A kid in a knight's costume crossed Lizzie's path. She snatched a plastic weapon from his armor.

"MA-ACE . . . good. . . ." moaned Lizzie. Gripping the weapon's sturdy handle, Lizzie swung the long chain until the ball of spikes at the end smashed into some nearby refreshments. Plates, cupcakes, and drinks went flying!

With a yelp, Kate and Miranda lunged toward the cafeteria doors.

"KA-ATE . . ." Lizzie continued to moan.

"Okay, this is the second-worst Halloween party I've even been to," said Miranda as she ran.

"KA-ATE . . . KA-ATE . . ."

Then Zombie-Clown Lizzie dropped the mace and slowly stalked after them, arms outstretched.

After Mr. and Mrs. McGuire finished their potpie dinners, Mr. McGuire clicked on the television.

"It's *Monster Chiller Horror Theater*," he told his wife with enthusiasm.

"Ooh, I'm very scared," said Mrs. McGuire, snuggling up to him on the couch. "You'd better hold me close."

"Okay, I'll, uh, protect you," said Mr. McGuire, putting his arm around her.

"That's right," she smiled.

"Mmm-hmm."

Just then, the doorbell rang. *Ding-dong!*

Mrs. McGuire frowned. "Don't get it," she told her husband. "They'll go away."

"Okay," agreed Mr. McGuire.

Ding-dong!

Ding-dong!

Ding-dong!

With a weary sigh, Mr. McGuire headed for the door.

"But we're out of candy," said Mrs. McGuire.

Mr. McGuire knew they were out of candy, all right. But he was hoping to come up with another giveaway "treat" before he reached the door.

Aha! he thought, spotting a coupon on the hall table. "Hey, no sweat, honey, we got a coupon from Burger Buddy for free French fries. Kids love fries."

Problem solved, thought Mr. McGuire as he pulled open the front door with a smile—and got hit *splat* in the face with a chicken potpie.

"Though they don't seem to be too fond of chicken potpie," he added with a sigh. Stunned, he just stood there—with peas, chicken, carrots, gravy, and crust totally dripping from his face and covering his shirt.

"Get some more candy bars next time, fatso!" cried the obnoxious kid.

From the living-room couch, Mrs. McGuire came running to her husband's side, totally offended by what had just happened.

"Hey," she yelled out the door, "that was good chicken potpie!"

CHAPTER SEVEN

Running for their lives through the halls of Hillridge Junior High, Miranda and Kate turned a corner and panicked, wondering where they should run to next.

"Let's hide in the dungeon," Miranda told Kate.

"Yes! Good!" said Kate. "We'll be safe in the dungeon!"

"KA-ATE . . ." moaned Lizzie, continuing to move toward them from the cafeteria.

"KA-ATE . . ."

Kate and Miranda screamed.

"KA-ATE . . ."

Together, Kate and Miranda rushed into the janitor's utility closet. It had been transformed into the dungeon of the Vampire mistress, with chains, bats, and scary-looking weapons hanging from hooks on the walls.

After Miranda and Kate rushed in, Miranda wedged a chair under the door handle.

"Okay, Lizzie is way out of line," said Kate, trying to catch her breath.

"She's *not* Lizzie right now," Miranda pointed out. "The spirits of the dead have taken over her body."

"KA-ATE . . ." Outside the closet, Zombie-Clown Lizzie moaned loudly and began to pound on the door. "KA-ATE!"

Miranda and Kate screamed.

"They're using Lizzie for . . . for revenge!"

Miranda told Kate. "They're mad because you called the Day of Dead artifacts stupid. And shoved them off in a little corner!"

As Zombie-Clown Lizzie continued to moan loudly, Kate hit her forehead with her fist. "Dumb Kate!" she muttered aloud to herself. "Dumb, dumb, dumb."

Zombie-Clown Lizzie's pounding grew louder, her moans more urgent. "KA-ATE! . . . KA-ATE . . . KA-ATE!"

"Can't we stop her?" Kate asked Miranda, nearly hysterical.

Miranda pressed her hand to her temples. "I *think* I remember my grandmother talking about ways to beg the spirits for forgiveness."

"KA-ATE! "

"We'll need a shovelful of graveyard dirt and a gallonful of blood," said Miranda. She and Kate immediately began to search the closet for anything resembling either.

"KA-ATE!"

"We're done for," said Kate, unable to find anything.

"No, no, no," said Miranda. "We don't need the actual stuff—it can be symbolic. There's chocolate cake and punch in the cafeteria—that can be the dirt and the blood."

"Great," said Kate. "What do we do?"

"We need to cover ourselves with it," said Miranda. "It shows our respect for the dead."

"KA-ATE!"

"No way," said Kate. "I am not going out there. At least we're safe in here."

She stepped backward, farther away from the closet door, when she felt a bony hand touch her shoulder. Kate turned to find the life-size skeleton bride and groom standing there, eyes glowing. The Day of the Dead skeletons were hiding right there with her, amid the dungeon junk!

Kate screamed "RUN!" and lunged for the closet door. Miranda was right behind her.

Fending off Zombie-Clown Lizzie with frantic slapping motions, the two girls bolted down the school hall.

"KA-ATE!" Lizzie moaned, following them.

Kate screamed as she burst through the cafeteria doors, Miranda bringing up the rear.

"You have to cover yourself with the punch and chocolate cake," Miranda reminded Kate.

Kate raced right over to the refreshments table. Without a second's pause, she dunked her head all the way into the punch bowl. Then she took handfuls of chocolate cake and smeared it all over herself.

The rest of the kids in the room stopped what they were doing and stared with disbelief as the Dungeon Mistress made a total spectacle of herself.

Suddenly, Zombie-Clown Lizzie appeared at the doorway, flanked by the skeleton bride and groom.

"KA-ATE!" moaned Zombie-Clown Lizzie.

"Miranda! It's not working!" cried Kate, seeing the creepy threesome heading her way.

"Okay, okay—now you have to perform the Dance of the Dead," said Miranda quickly. "Twirl around and hop on one foot."

Kate did.

"Now caw like a crow," added Miranda.

"Caw! Caw! Caw! Caw! Caw! Caw!" screeched Kate, hopping around in a circle. Punch dripped from her hair, chocolate cake crumbs rolled down her back.

Suddenly, Matt appeared out of the crowd and said, "Now, pat the top of your head and swat your rump."

Kate was so caught up in the "ritual," she

didn't even notice it was *Matt* who'd spoken. As she continued to hop on one foot, she began to pat her head and swat her rump.

Lizzie then stepped closer and said in a perfectly normal voice, "Now, say, 'Lizzie, Lizzie, please forgive me.'"

"Lizzie, Lizzie," began Kate. Then she stopped and looked up. "*What?*"

That's when Gordo stepped forward, digital video camera in hand, and added, "Now say 'cheese.'"

Gordo snapped Kate's photo just as she realized she'd been had.

"Aw, this will look terrific in the school newspaper," said Gordo.

He set down the camera, attached a tiny speaker to it, retreated a few steps, and produced the radio microphone he'd used to throw his voice.

"Help me, I'm going to look ridiculous on

the front page, *agghhhh!*" said Gordo into the device.

His voice sounded high and tinny—just like when it had come out of the Burger Buddy toy.

As Kate realized how she'd been fooled, it also dawned on her that the entire room of kids was now laughing and pointing at her.

There was nothing Kate could say. She just stood there with her punch-soaked hair and cake-covered face.

"What's the matter, Kate?" asked Miranda. "Zombie got your tongue?"

With a smile, Miranda then turned to the bride and groom skeletons. "Thanks, Mom, thanks, Dad."

The bride and groom removed their skeletal faces. Behind the masks were the faces of Miranda's *parents*!

Kate's jaw dropped in surprise.

"*De nada,* sweetheart," Mrs. Sanchez told her daughter.

"I told you the Day of the Dead was my favorite holiday," said Mr. Sanchez with a chuckle.

"Now, you have fun with Lizzie tonight," Mrs. Sanchez told Miranda, planting a kiss on her daughter's cheek, "and we'll see you tomorrow."

After Mr. and Mrs. Sanchez left, Miranda grinned at Kate and gave her a little wave.

Completely humiliated, Kate groaned and ran for the door.

Lizzie laughed as Matt hopped around, cawing. Then she, Miranda, and Gordo all high-fived one another.

Nasty, superior Kate had finally been taken down a few notches—at least, for the moment.

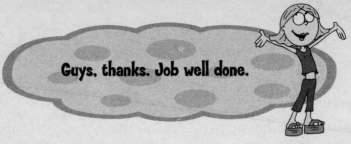

Guys, thanks. Job well done.

Back at the McGuire house, the tricks of Halloween weren't quite over yet.

After Mr. McGuire had changed out of his chicken-potpie-covered shirt, he went to the backyard and pulled the garden hose all the way into the house's front entryway.

At the same time, Mrs. McGuire rummaged through the kitchen pantry and brought out a big carton of raw oatmeal.

"You really think he's gonna come back?" asked Mrs. McGuire, lifting the lid off the oatmeal.

"Hey, I was a kid once. I know how these punks think," said Mr. McGuire.

Just then, the doorbell rang.

"See, right on cue!" said Mr. McGuire,

putting his finger on the trigger of the hose's spray nozzle. "So, uh, on the count of three?"

"Yeah."

"One. Two."

As the doorbell continued to ring, Lizzie's parents scurried forward. Then Mrs. McGuire yanked open the door and Mr. McGuire shouted, "Trick-or-treat, ya punk!"

As Mr. McGuire let loose the full force of his garden hose, Mrs. McGuire stepped up and chucked the oatmeal forward.

For a moment, they were gleeful. Revenge sure felt sweet—especially on Halloween night!

But then they stopped, appalled, and stepped backward into the hallway.

"Aaaah! Oh!" cried Mrs. McGuire, seeing what they'd just done—and, more important, *who* they'd just done it to.

Miranda's parents stood on the McGuires' front porch. They were soaked, covered with oatmeal—and completely confused.

"Miranda's staying over tonight, and she forgot her sleeping bag," Mr. Sanchez explained with remarkable politeness.

"Oh. Oh!" cried Mrs. McGuire, horrified. "We thought you were a trick-or-treater."

"I see," said Mrs. Sanchez, calmly wiping oatmeal out of her eyes. "We give them *candy* at our house."

Mr. McGuire looked totally mortified. "I'll get a towel," he said, then dashed off.

"I'll go make some coffee!" said Mrs. McGuire and dashed off, too.

As the Sanchezes stood dripping in the entryway, Mr. Sanchez just shook his head. Then he turned to his wife and said, "Told you we should have called first."

This was one Halloween that Lizzie, her friends, and their parents wouldn't be forgetting anytime soon!

Don't close the book on Lizzie yet!
Here's a sneak peek at the next
Lizzie McGuire story. . . .

Adapted by Alice Alfonsi
Based on the series created by Terri Minsky
Based on a teleplay written by Melissa Gould

Something was definitely up.

The Hillridge Junior High cheerleaders
were being nice—and not just to the jocks.
The pom-pom princesses were talking to

every kid they passed in the cafeteria, regardless of their dorkiness level.

"Hey! Hi!" said Kate Sanders, smiling at Harvey Barnes, a Mathlete with acne issues. The poor kid almost fainted from shock.

"Hi, nice to meet you!" Claire Miller gushed to Janice Baxter, a shy, gawky girl who was secretary of the Audiovisual Club.

Before today, Claire never even *glanced* at an "uncool" person like Janice. Now she was treating the girl like a long-lost cousin . . . or a *sibling* even!

Time for a reality check, Lizzie McGuire thought. She leaned toward her best friend, Miranda Sanchez, who was sitting across from her at their usual lunchroom table. "Okay, something's going on. Claire is being nice—to *everybody*—and Kate's not even stopping her."

Miranda nodded. "Tell me about it. She

actually said hi to *me* this morning."

Lizzie watched Kate and Claire continue their gushfest, from table to table, all the way across the cafeteria. This was totally unbelievable. The Hillridge cafeteria wasn't just some big, uncharted landmass where you ate your lunch. It was a region with very specific territories. There was Cool-ville, Normal Land, and at least three levels of Dorkdom. And Kate and Claire were doing the unthinkable—crossing every single border! When they reached the corner table against the back wall, Lizzie's jaw dropped.

"Claire is talking to the dorkestra!" Lizzie blurted.

Claire, the witchiest snob in school, was giving props to a girl who carried her lunch around in a violin case! And Kate was practically flirting with Felix Martin, a kid who once had a piece of sheet music taped to his back for three entire periods before he even noticed!

"They must've lost a dare," Miranda said.

Lizzie wasn't so sure. And then, her other best friend, David "Gordo" Gordon, sat down with his lunch tray and cleared it all up.

"This just in," he reported. "Claire is running for class president."

"No wonder," said Lizzie.

"It's so unfair," said Miranda. "Claire's going to end up our class president, and it's only because she's popular."

"The popular kids win everything," Lizzie said with a sigh. "It's been that way since kindergarten. The rest of us are just doomed."

As Miranda nodded in agreement, something caught her eye. Her eyebrows rose, and her features scrunched up into an expression of confusion and horror. "Uhm, you guys?

Why is Larry Tudgeman eating *worms?*"

Lizzie and Gordo followed Miranda's gaze to a table deep in the land of Dorkdom. Two kids were staring at Larry, who was dangling a worm close to his open mouth.

"Oh, Larry's running, too," Gordo explained with a shrug. "He said he'd eat one worm for every person who votes for him."

Lizzie shuddered as Larry dropped the squirming earthworm into his mouth. Why was Tudgeman always such a . . . *Tudgeman?*

Miranda grimaced. "That's kind of desperate. Not to mention, gross."

"And very unfair to the worms," Lizzie pointed out.

"Great choice," said Gordo rolling his eyes in disgust. "Claire or Tudgeman." Then he thought about it a moment and said, "Why doesn't anyone *normal* run? Like us."

"One of *us* run?" Miranda put her hand on

Gordo's forehead. "Are you feeling okay?"

"It could work. We're not popular, but we don't *need* to be. We are . . . the normals!" Gordo declared.

Lizzie looked at Miranda, then at Gordo. *Huh?*

"There are more of us than there are of them," he explained, getting more excited by the second. "If we can just get everyone to vote for a *normal* candidate, we could win!"

"You think?" Miranda asked hopefully.

Gordo nodded enthusiastically.

Wow, thought Lizzie. Gordo is really onto something!

Yeah, let's overthrow the ruling powers!

"Which is why I nominate *you*, Lizzie McGuire!" Gordo announced.

Lizzie's eyes widened in shock. "Me?"

Miranda blinked. It took her a second to get used to the idea, but once she did, she said, "He's right. You're, like, *totally* normal."

Lizzie frowned at Miranda.

"That's a good thing," Miranda assured her.

"You guys are joking," said Lizzie. "I am not . . . am I?"

"You have what it takes," said Gordo. "You're one of the normals. *You* could be our class president!"

"You could be . . . the voice of the people!" said Miranda, with her hand extended dramatically as if she were presenting Lizzie to her adoring public.

The voice of the people, Lizzie repeated to herself. That actually sounded kind of cool—not to mention the idea of an adoring public.

Suddenly, Lizzie saw herself running for higher office. Representative Lizzie McGuire . . . Senator Lizzie McGuire . . . President of the United States—Lizzie McGuire . . . For a second, she actually wondered if Mount Rushmore had enough room for one more face.

"Okay, I'll do it," Lizzie told her friends, suddenly sure of herself. "I *will* run for Class President!"

Of course, once she'd actually *said* it, she suddenly *wasn't* so sure anymore.

i don't have a good feeling about this.

Sorry! That's the end of the sneak peek for now. But don't go nuclear! To read the rest, all you have to do is look for the next title in the Lizzie McGuire series—

Lizzie for PRESIDENT

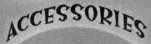